GLOOMY
SUMMER

by

Annabella Baker

Disclaimer

GLOOMY SUMMER

"Eastern songs are more beautiful, and anyone with a heart who listens to them will be moved to tears."

-Joseph Roth

Acknowledgments

Thanks to my husband for his precious support

Thanks to Déryné Bisztró for allowing me to bring it into my story

Many thanks to the photographer Benjamin Kövesi for the fantastic job in catching the essence of my book

To my beloved grandmother Marina

..and to all my Hungarian friends

Table of Contents

Introduction

Alexandra, also known as Sasha, is a beautiful châtain clair-haired and brown-eyed woman. Two rows of perfect milky white teeth and a nose that sat elegantly on her oval face. Not tall, friendly, but not totally outgoing. She carried herself with dignity that only aristocracy can bestow on a person. Her lashes, long and curly, protected her beautiful eyes, and even though she was pretty unassuming, she was also a presence that was intimidating enough to make people listen.

Inside, she was a cold weather lover. Long winters held an appeal that no other weather did. Her couch, blanket, and an excellent novel were all she needed. All of these were saliently different from her background. So different indeed that she begins to doubt the authenticity at a very early age. She is a determined, well-mannered, hardworking, albeit somewhat nostalgic and confused human. This is excusable because of reasons that will only be discovered through reading this text, but when we dare to ask whether or not it has or will make any difference in her life, it remains to be seen in what she does with the new life that she had been offered.

What makes a person? Is it nature...or is it nurture? Is it based on how they were raised or based on genetics? Scientists and researchers often disagree on this topic. And even though we generally do not have memories of the time before we were born, or even the first few years after, there are some people who happen to be conscious of who they are. For example, we often say that children may have preferences for specific music, mainly if their parents listened to it, usually when carrying them.

We find solace in beauty, truth, and the songs that appeal to our souls. It is a gentle reminder of the power we have in us to be emotive.

How much impact our pre-conscious experience has on our behaviours and attitude to life. This book explores these multiple possibilities.

The story is a product of observation, questions, and an active imagination that developed a sense of appreciation and respect for other cultures while staying strictly true to mine.

It's a real page-turner and would keep you fascinated until the end.

With this in mind, our story begins on the streets of Budapest. A city where our central character, a forty-year-old beauty with light brown hair and dark chocolate eyes, contrasted very sharply with her milky, pale skin. Anyone who looked into her eyes found an intense attraction every single time. She travels between neighbouring countries because that is what she wants to do. And in a country where she would otherwise be a stranger, she becomes a tour guide. Her journeys would take her through towns, villages, and cities, and though she does stop to take a breath and rest, it rarely ever lasts for more than a few days at a time. The nomad life felt right to her, and while she was unsure why she rarely wanted to be anything but on the road, she embraced the life and decided to be a tour guide, amongst other things such as a book reader, an event organiser, and a dancer when she was in the mood. She didn't do any of these things for money; while she would get paid, she often gave it away for good causes because her bills were paid before she even knew they existed. Fancy having met, sat with, and been led across town by a multi-millionaire guide and not knowing the better? But the story isn't about her money...

The story questions what we are at the very core of our existence. How far precisely has biology brought us? Far enough to have memories before we are born? In our DNA? Do we know things intuitively, or is there just information in our DNA that reminds us of our ancestors' lives and attempts to help us retain our link to them by steering us in specific directions?

Part 1

Budapest, April

The tour bus rocked just a little and bounced just a little as it moved through the city of Budapest. She stood in it, smiling, gesturing, and showing the eager eyes that surrounded her, everything that mattered. This was what she loved to do, this was how she enjoyed life, and while it did pay some good amount of money, she knew that she would still get up, get dressed, and go to work even if the money stopped coming. Cool air got into her hair. Her brown eyes glowed, the streets of Budapest reflecting in her eyes. Her favourite part of most tours was the Citadella upon the Gellért Hill. Tourists were taken aback by the beauty of the fortress; breath-taking view over the Danube and the whole city. It didn't matter that she had been there a hundred times over. She always marvelled at the beauty of the river. It took her breath away every single time. Presently, the tour bus had just arrived at Heroes' Square.

She repeated the location in Hungarian because to her ears sounded more melodic. To Sasha, the Hungarian language was going straight to her heart like when you are in love for the very first time.

She turned to her tourists and said with a bright smile:

"Now you are about to see some of Budapest's most beautiful and historical arts. To our far left is the Museum of Fine Arts, and here to our right is the Hall of Art..." her voice was clear and strong.

The tourists loved what they were seeing, and that was obvious in how they quickly got their smartphones and started to take pictures.

"You most likely won't be allowed to take pictures in the museums..." she said, but nobody seemed to be listening at that moment. She smiled, knowing that most of them would not listen to her, but the security at the museums would make them put their devices away for the duration of their inner museum tour. When they got back, she was ready with some new intriguing stories and facts about their next destination.

It was the State Opera House and the magnificent Andrassy Avenue, and they were instantly excited.

People stood around and listened to her. They laughed at her jokes. They interacted with her questions, and when it was all done, they tipped her extra. She accepted gratefully and never rejected even once, mostly because she believed that a worker deserves his wages, but there was also something in the way people on tour give gifts. Because she knew they appreciated her excellent tailor-made tours. Listening to the great history of a beautiful nation and its people, never her talks were dull or tedious. On the contrary, her tours were exciting, inspiring, and delivered with passion.

Of all the cities she loved to visit from her birth country, Italy, Budapest stood out to her. The city of Budapest always held a special fascination for her. She loved it there. But it wasn't just about the architecture or the beauty. It was also about the fact that she felt like she belonged there. It was about familiarity.

She could remember one time when she heard a Hungarian song in a taxi; even though she had no idea what the words meant, they actually spoke to her soul so well that she started to cry; a profound feeling that was coming from deep inside her heart. Something she had never felt before.

There is another day. Another bus. With her pale, fair hair that flows down her back and reaches tentatively towards her waist, she stood in the middle...this time pointing at the beautiful Liberty Bridge, showing the elegance of the Parliament, identifying the famous Market Hall at the end of Váci Street, naming things all over town. Something about those houses, figures, stories and trees held a unique interaction with her. She loved Budapest, but it was not just about the fact that she had found a lot of fun. It was something in the air. The calm, the breeze, the way everything would fall silent in the evenings. It was about the long, lonely walks she took and the stories and gossip that that city gave her, like an old friend. It was about the fact that the food appealed to her; the smells took her back to distant memories. And each time she sat down in a restaurant, there was a rush of excitement. But perhaps what stood out to her the most was the fact that she picked up the language so fast. She had come to Budapest as a student on an excursion. And she had decided that this was where she wanted to visit, a lot... Her parents tried many times to convince her to come home and stay home. The house was imposing, standing on the beautiful hills on the outskirts of Venice, and she was the heiress to it. Her grandparents had lost two of their three children when they were younger. And now her father was the heir to all the estate. And if her father died, she would be the heiress of all that estate. It was a very well-known vineyard where the fruity, tangy white wine was at its finest. It sounded like a good reason to be back home, facing the family business and just growing her wealth and enjoying life. But even though everything a person could want was available in that house, she still didn't want it. It was a delicate balance as she didn't feel like she deserved it and didn't believe that anybody needed that much space or wealth. But perhaps, most important was the fact that her mind was somewhere else. Her soul and her desires were in a different City. She didn't even need to think too hard to know what she wanted.

The things she read about Budapest stuck in her brain. She did not have to read repeatedly. She did not have to try to remember anything about Hungarian history actively. Was it said to her? When?

To some extent, she felt like it was some sort of instinct. Has she lived in Budapest before, in a previous life? She knew the city, and she felt like its people knew her, and together they had built a special relationship. A bond that not even the concept of the family could break. By the time she had spent a little short than a year in Budapest, she was able to speak and write Hungarian fluently. It did not feel as though she was learning a new language. Instead, it felt as though she remembered a language she had always known before. There was a time when she used to tell people that she was not even native to the city, but these days she didn't even bother because they didn't believe her anyway.

Another thing she particularly loved about Budapest was the rain... If she was walking out in the city and the rain started to pour, she would intentionally slow down such that the rain would drench her. A wet Budapest was a loved Budapest for her. The smell of the elements in the air was something that she could not resist. Autumn was the most attractive season for her. Above all, however, was the fact that Budapest gave her a feeling of acceptance. She often wanted to hug people... tell everyone that she loved them and their country. In her mind, they felt the same. This was how it was going to be. Budapest loved her as much as she loved it. Sasha knew that it was home, but nothing served as a resounding affirmation better than the fact that the people seemed to accept her wholeheartedly too. She never felt like a visitor, bit even once. Every visit was a homecoming.

As the bus approached their last destination for the day, her phone started to ring. It was her old grandmother on the phone. She never saved the house phone, but she recognized the number every time.

"Nana..." She said into the phone.

"Alexandra, my baby!!!" the caring, calm voice of the grandmother came over the phone. Alexandra immediately smiled.

Her Grandmother loved her; it was obvious. But Grandad would call her a million pet names if she let him.

"How are you, Nana?" she asked, pursing her lips in a failed attempt at not sounding like she was in a hurry to get her grandmother off the phone.

"I'll be fine if my only granddaughter would just call me a little more!" it was a blatant accusation. She sighed inwards and tried to smile.

"I'm sorry, Nana," Alexandra said. There was a brief silence over the phone, and then grandma said:

"Did your parents tell you that they would be coming over for two weeks?" Sasha shook her head even though her granny could not see it at that moment.

"They didn't tell me anything."

"Well, now I'm telling you." There was silence over the phone. One that they were both familiar with. Her grandmother knew quite well that a big part of why she didn't like to go home was often an unspoken tension between her and her parents.

"… and I want you to come. I want you to come home, Alexandra," her Nana's voice came over the phone.

"Nana…"

"don't argue with me, child. You want me to die without seeing my only grandchild again?" She decided it was time to visit home again. Now, as she stood with the phone to her ear, she felt that slow tightening of her chest that reminded her of all the things she would rather forget.

"Did you hear me, young lady?" Nana's voice came again. She cleared her throat slightly.

"Yes, Nana."

Alexandra turned back to the people in her tour party with that infectious smile.

"So now who is ready to see the beautiful New York Café?" she asked, and they all clapped their hands. With Alexandra, this was the norm. And this was her happy place.

Outskirts of Venice, May

The cloud gathered the distance. Thick and bold like that stroke of colours she put on the canvas in art class. The rain beat her, like literally hitting her as she feebly tried to move up the hill. She loved the rain on her skin and the heavy breeze on her face. Going up that hill in that rain reminded her of the good times. Those days when she was just a little girl, with her little hand enclosed in her grandmother's, walking up the seemingly never-ending hill or down the same hill a little too fast. Her wet hair smelt like the rich, exotic, and very expensive lavender shampoo that her mother used for her. She always smiled when she climbed that hill in the rain because there was a feeling it gave her, a feeling that she could not explain in words, nor was she ever willing to. That feeling was hers to own and to cherish. It was the one thing that she was so sure of in the midst of all the other weird thoughts that sat grandly in the palace of her little mind. In those good old days, she would have on those little red wellies that she loved so much instead of the high-heeled sandals that she presently had on. She had been only three, but she remembered very well that walk as she used to do it every day going to nursery with her babysitter.

Alice.

Alice was a great babysitter. Alexandra remembered twirling her small chubby kid hands through her beautiful long blonde hair. Alice was tall, funny, and always ready with the umbrella if it started to rain. She was her one true love as a child because they were close. They did everything together. There was nothing in Alexandra's life that she shared exclusively with her parents or even grandparents. But the one thing that stood out to her particularly was the stark differences in how she saw and enjoyed life versus how her parents did.

She was only three when she realised that the sun was too hot for her, too bright for her eyes, and the summer far too long. There was nothing to do on those long summer days when her parents were taking her to the beach, to those expensive posh holidays where kids are scarce and the parents party all night. The ideal holiday for her parents. The perfect boredom for her.

She's happy when it is winter and the days are shorter. When is cold and misty. When the sun doesn't show its stupid face for months. When the warm yellow streetlight shines on the cold nights. The lights barely led through the fog, but she loved the sight of it all the same. She would find herself just sitting on her windowsill and looking longingly at the fog and the tiny spec of light that hung inside it.

The days passed by, between sand castles and walks with Alice. Her parents seemed to enjoy their summer days. She wondered whether she would ever be as excited about summer as they were. But this was not the only thing she wondered about. She wondered about the drastic physical differences between her parents and herself. Her father, a tall, dignified man with a quiet, aristocratic air around him, was a man of few words. His shoulders were squared at all times, and his back was straight. From the time she was a little girl, she always remembered him having a little grey in his hair. It was in the same place, just a little above his sideburns. And his skin was slightly tanned... even in winter when there was no sun. Her mother was also tall. She barely looked like she had even been pregnant. She looked like a runway model who had retired but had never changed her lifestyle. She was always looking perfectly made up, her hair never looked out of place, and her nails were always just perfect. The way they talked, the way they ate, walked, the way they carried themselves generally... Alexandra always felt out of place. She wasn't as concerned with her looks as they were, and she definitely wasn't tall or skinny. The differences remained stark and obvious to her, even though nobody else seemed to see it.

Presently, she finished climbing the hill and took a deep breath. She was used to the terrain, but she made a severe mistake thinking she could climb the hill with her high-heeled sandals. She had decided because she wanted to reminisce on the good old days when she used to climb the hill with her babysitter or one of her grandparents. She could see the sprawling lawns around the big mansion that housed her grandparents. The property had been in the family for generations. A wonderful Champs Elysees of cypresses (like grandma called it) led to the Villa.

A beautiful mansion with so many shutters.

She bent over and undid the straps of the high-heeled sandals that had been the source of gross discomfort for most of her uphill journey.

She heard laughter coming from inside. Nana was there... she could hear her voice, her rich, sweet melody of a voice. Sasha's chest suddenly felt tight. She knew her parents were there too. It was why she had come home.

She decided to wait till they either came out or walked further into the house before going in. She wanted to get a chance to walk those long hallways on her own, glare at her ancestors, and maybe ask their still, high achieving selves some questions to see if they would answer. She stood there, counting backward from a hundred. Memories filled her head to bursting point. The long holidays shared with her grandparents... Those had been good. But the winters ... The winters were the best. Staying indoors all day long, reading a book, or playing cards with Grandad.

She walked into the hallway and knew what was coming- the assault of a familiar scent on her nostrils and the instant plunge down memory lane.

The hallway was filled with pictures of multiple generations of her ancestors. The family had been wealthy for generations now, but it wasn't just that. It was also the fact that this family seemed to look almost the same over generations. Children almost always looked like someone in the family, and the gene was that strong, strong enough for nearly every child of the family to spot one of either the trademark deep blue eyes of the majority of the family members. The nose... the cheekbones... even the smile seemed pretty consistent across the board. It was never difficult to tell cousins even before they get introduced. And this was part of the reasons Alexandra would stand in front of the mirror for minutes unending, trying to find at least one thing that linked her to her parents other than a birth certificate. Something biological, something obvious. Her hair was different, so were her eyes and lips and her nose... her nose definitely couldn't come from the family. Not to add that she was the opposite of everything they were.

As she walked down the hall ever so slowly, her bare feet now walking on the wooden floors, very comfortable as they sunk into the luxury of the floors that made no sound, with her pretty flowery floating dress, she stared into eyes after eyes. Waiting for that moment when she would identify someone in the family hallway... someone with whom she would share some affinity, connection, or some form of resemblance. She bit down on her lower lip and sighed. The issues had actively ridden her mind for years, literally since she had been around four years old and even more so now.

Part 2

Family gathering

She turned around, and her grandmother stood there. Old, frail, but ever straight in that regal position and her short silver hair that she remembered so vividly. She carried herself with dignity and had so much fewer wrinkles than the average woman of her age would be expected to have. She wore a delicate blue dress that descended just a little below the knees. Her smile was beautiful, and her eyes glinted in the hallway as she glared at her granddaughter. Everyone that saw pictures of her from when she was young knew that she was the goddess of smiles. Sasha's father had inherited that smile, and his wife often mentioned it whenever she talked about how they met. The smile was definitely one of the reasons she first noticed him. Things that she wished she had. These were things that she coveted heavily in her family if nothing is.

Presently those amazing eyes were staring at her with the glints.

"I thought you wouldn't come!" She spoke. Sasha rolled her eyes with a smile. Of course, she would come; her nana had called... who would dare say no?

"Nana..." Alexandra said with a smile.

The old woman's arms came up, and Alexandra walked into them gently, resting her head on the woman's shoulder and taking in a deep lungful of her preferred perfume, 'Soir de Paris.'

"I missed you so much," Alexandra said while kissing her as she rested her head on her grandmother's shoulder ever so gently, making sure not to put her weight on the older woman.

"I missed you too, my darling." nana said.

"Come... Get washed up and come down to dinner. You look like you crawled through a chimney to get here." Alexandra laughed. Her grandmother never ceased to make her laugh... She was funny in a delicate way. It was one of the few things that she enjoyed about being a family member. She took the arm that her grandmother offered and instantly got flooded with memories. Memories of walking with her and granddad on the other side and holding the other hand. She remembered the two older people raising her in unison, allowing her feet to dangle. She remembered shrieking because the feeling was like flowing through the air and then landing on the floor on both feet almost immediately. Grandma, now she was so much older, her fingers twisted and curled like roots of an old tree, and deep down, she wished that her grandparents were still strong enough to lift her together.

"Go on up... Go wash up," her grandmother said again. High heeled shoes in her hands and feet aching, she padded up the stairs and went straight to the room that had her name on the door for over two decades.

At the top of the stairs, she paused and looked down into the living room. The aristocratic elegance was beautiful to see. And despite the annual redecorating projects, everything in the house was familiar... The curtains started from the edge of the ceiling and gently touched the floor. The room was done in a regal mixture of green, gold, and a bold, confident red in very strategic places. The chairs were carefully carved, with every other piece of furniture looking like it was specially handcrafted for the family. The small flag with the family crest hung from a wall in permanently graceful flight. The room smelled of expensive diffusers and fresheners. The scent was pleasant but just a little too strong for her.

Her room was the same except for the bigger, more age-appropriate bed. The colour though recently redone, was precisely the same. The bedding was a sweet shade of pink, but every other thing was either a sweet pale cream or off-white. There was an occasional dash of wine colour here and there, but the room was predominantly that pale, calming colour that made her instantly want to lie down and sleep. This was one of the perks of being born to a wealthy family. Her room had been designed specially. The simple elegance was definitely not her parent's style. If her parents had their way, her room would be done in a million colours, and she would have the most expensive furnishing that money could buy. But her grandparents had given her some free rein with the room and every time she wanted to add or remove something, they just nodded and called in the designer to have the conversation with her and help her get exactly what she wanted. It had to be nice, of course... But there were no specific rules about it being expensive... Which was a plus.

While she liked having comfort, there were just too many parts of being rich that she didn't quite like. She didn't like the fixation on being a certain way, especially when it came to etiquette, attitude, outlook on life, the life she had to live, and everything else.

It was more about the fact that she did not feel like she belonged to this world, to those who adored her like her parents. As much as she tried to like the things they did, she could not bring herself to. And it was more than just a feeling. It felt more like knowing that she did not belong to them, either biologically or otherwise. She looked around the room. One last time and she stepped into the shower. She needed to freshen up before she went downstairs to see her family. She sat there on her bed and multiple flashbacks rushed through her mind. One of the strongest memories that filled her mind was the one when she was a little girl, and she was having a sleepover at her friend Ella's home. They had been getting ready for bed when Ella walked into the room with her hair flowing down her shoulders.

She had startling green eyes and red hair that was always brushed to smooth perfection.

"Your hair is so cute!" Sasha had said to her friend.

"It's just like my mammy's," she said. It was a clear statement, but it still left six-year-old Alexandra feeling sideways because she was old enough to know that she could not attribute any of her features to either of her parents.

Presently, she took a moment to wonder if her father had ever gotten teased about the fact that his only child looked so different from him by his friends. She wondered if anyone had ever said something and how her parents handled the situation. As she got ready, she made a mental note to ask her father that question. Someone must have said something, and people weren't that nice that they would never have gossiped. She was now ready to take on things.

Part 3

Reminiscences

There was the first clap of thunder as she looked at the clock in the extreme hand of the room and saw that it was almost 7:00 PM. The thunderstorms were always lovely and heavy. Oh, how much she loved the sound of the rain crashing into her windows and shutters. She used to be scared of them when she was a child, but these days she had come to find comfort in thunderstorms because her best memories were made in them. They reminded her of the time she spent with her grandfather, playing in the garden or planting flowers. There was a smell that always came with thunderstorms on the mountains. And if a person decided to take a walk in the woods just after that thunderstorm, there was a feeling that came with that smell. There was no single word to describe the feeling. It was a combination of sounds, sight, impressions, sensations, and emotions. It was the smell and sound of the pine cones when they fell on the wet path.

The smell of the soil when the rain brushes away all the pine needles. It was the noise of your steps in the silent wood, where the only sound is the echo of your voice, but all is muffled. There was also the cracking of a few trees and her grandfather's ethereal voice, a man of very few words. When she was a child, he spoke more, mostly when he taught her the different names of trees and how not to get lost in the woods. His tall, slender frame seemed like a natural part of the forest, and it might as well have been. The man could spot a disturbance in the soil, leaves, and literally everything around him from a reasonable distance away.

"Alexandra, are you there?" her mother's voice came to her. She sighed and checked herself out in the mirror even though she was fresh out of the shower. She was still concerned about how she looked and what her mother thought of it.

"Yes... yes, mam... I'm in here". The door opened, and her mother walked in, splendid, tall, and beautiful as always. She was wearing a red dress long and elegant.

"You didn't bother to say hello to anyone in the house!" her mother said. For as long as Sasha knew her mother, she had never known her to be overweight or even slightly so. She always looked impeccable. From the curve of her eyebrows to the shoes she wore. She always looked flawless, even in bed and when she had just gotten out.

"I thought that everyone was busy, and we will meet at dinner anyway." She spoke. Her mother looked at her and said:

"Are you still wearing that silly bracelet? It wasn't a question... nor was it a statement for that matter.

"YES! I love it, and it means a lot to me...."

The bracelet in question, beautifully made, had roses painted on a single small porcelain bead, probably very cheap but rich in meaning, had been given to her years back by a lady in Budapest unknown to her. This woman in her late 50s, who owned a patisserie in Budapest Oktogon, told her to keep it.

"It's yours like this country."

She never really understood the meaning of those words but those words are still resounding now more than ever before.

The question had never been whether or not her parents loved her. If they didn't, they did a superb job hiding the fact. The question was that despite all the love and affection shown by her entire family, she still constantly felt like she didn't belong there.

"Are you coming?"

Alexandra was instantly drawn out of her reverie. She blinked a couple of times and looked in the direction the sound came from.

"Yes, yes, I'm coming now." She said with a small sigh as she followed her mother down the staircase. There was so much to remember in this house. Most of her good childhood memories were made in this house, on this property. And while she was grateful for them, she wished that she had made even more memories.

She walked into the room with a straight face. She couldn't help but wonder how it was so easy for her parents to ignore the things she was saying at the time. She had expressed her doubts about her own paternity on many separate occasions, and her parents had brushed it aside. Did it ever occur to them that it was abnormal for a child to be entirely unlike the parents? Yes, there were many ways that genetics could have formed itself and expressed itself. But what were the odds that a couple that looked that way would produce a child that looked absolutely the opposite of them, and how would they explain the fact that she never seems to be able to key into their way of life or get used to their likes and dislikes?

It wasn't quite expected that children that were born into a household would completely alienate themselves from such homes. So, what exactly were they thinking?

She had many reasons to love her parents. And perhaps many more reasons to adore and respect them. But this was one thing that she found it challenging to come to terms with. She knew that questions were to be asked, even as a little girl. How come nobody else seemed to know this? Didn't they ever look at her and wonder where she might have come from in the family lineage? Perhaps it definitely didn't help very much that she didn't have siblings to compare herself to. But even so, she had cousins. And there was a specific trend that was common to all her cousins that did not apply to her in any way. That in itself should have been a source for questioning.

The minute she walked into the house and got greeted by her grandmother, everything changed. All she felt was love. Love for these people who took her in and never once questioned all her features. They never treated her differently or unkindly just because she looked different. No matter what, she was the apple of their eyes. And even though she constantly brought up the possibility of them not being her biological parent, it never occurred to them to check. And here she was, a fully grown woman who had never had to worry or wonder where anything was ever going to come from.

As she sat down for dinner, her father reached for her hand and held it in that sweet loving manner as he always did.

She clearly remembered a night like this, at a dinner table, a far too long dinner table just like this, where she had asked her parents directly if she was adopted with inside that fear of discovering the truth. But was she really prepared to know the truth, even if it's painful? To hear that yes, she has been adopted but she's very much loved. Or maybe that her biological parents are dead?

Did she want to discover that? Her heartbeat was going so fast but she decided to go ahead with her plan regardless.

Because she had a plan!

If she had been adopted, she would still carry on as usual, but at least she would know the truth and why she is so different. If her real biological parents were dead, then she would have at least a grave to lay pretty flowers.

She wished to have a photo of them and their address. Maybe they were still alive but didn't want her. Maybe she looked like them.

Her parents had laughed.

"Why would you even think so, sweetheart? "Her father asked.

"I mean… I don't really look like either of you… neither do I look like anyone in our extended family… haven't you ever wondered why?"

Her father had stared at her for a few moments to contemplate what to do with her. And then:

"Sasha, my dear… have you heard the word genetics?

Genetics is just the study of hereditary markers and their expressions in the human body". The issue with her father was that once he decided to start talking about something, he would not stop until he got his point across.

"Well, in genetics, there's something called recessive gene. And there's also something called dominant gene. There are some traits that may not manifest for several generations in a family. But at the end of the day, these traits can all come together and manifest at just once. It doesn't mean you are adopted; it just means you have a combination of recessive traits from multiple generations of my family and your mother".

His explanation ought to have been OK, but it wasn't. And when she looked to her mother for some support, her mother just sat down there and laughed.

"So, my dear, you are not adopted. You are my little bundle of joy."

Her mother had said.

"If you want us to show you your baby pictures straight from the hospital. You were so pink I actually thought there was something wrong with you. They took you straight to the neonatal intensive care unit because of your low birth weight. It took several reassurances from the doctors in order for me to believe that my baby was fine. My pregnancy was exceedingly difficult, so we agreed not to have more babies. Otherwise, maybe you would have been lucky enough to have siblings who actually look as different as you.

Sasha remained quiet for the rest of the dinner, trying to process everything her parents had said to her. They did not seem to be lying, and she had every reason to believe them. But each time she walked past and caught her face in the mirror, she just could not bring herself to believe them completely. Something had been off. She had known it as a little girl.

That evening, after dinner, they all sat down with the huge family photo album, memories, cakes, and laughter. There were pictures after pictures of her as an infant. There were pictures of her mother pregnant. And pictures of her in hospital.

"You know, you did not sleep much in the first months," her father said as he took another slice of cake.

If nothing else, she could hear the emotions in her father's voice. She knew that he was telling the truth.

The conversation persisted, but she stopped hearing the words and became absorbed in her parent's faces. They both looked so animated as they talked about her as a child.

"When she was young, we couldn't wait for her to be grown. And now..." her father looked at her with love in his eyes. Alexandra looked away. There was so much that she wanted to say and do. In moments like that, she felt like a complete idiot for daring even to wonder if she had been born to this family.

Very ungrateful, that's how she felt; after all the love and affection her parents are showing her every day, how can she be so insensitive and stupid to ask or even doubt.

.Apologising for her silliness, she went on with her everyday life until her mid-thirties, forgetting all about it. Only on a few rare occasions did a subtle doubt come to the surface of her heart, but she carries on, known to be unfounded.

That day at the table was the last time Sasha actively asked her parents questions about her birth. They had too many details, and it all seemed to add up and she just did not have the heart to start that conversation again as it was apparently something that her parents were sensitive about.

Looking at them now, in their silver years and looking happy and fulfilled, she did not want to take that away from them, nor did she want to cause unnecessary upset to her grandparents.

Her grandfather already did not come downstairs much anymore. When he was younger, he used to carry her on his shoulders everywhere. He would call her "love of my life" in that exquisitely Italian manner. She was his partner in crime, his friend... More like his best friend, he just showered her with the best of everything she wanted. She thought that maybe it was because she was his only grandchild, but the more she grew, the more she realized that grandad was the one person she really connected with in the house. He listened to her, really listened. He never laughed at her unless she made a joke, but perhaps the most important thing was that he never dismissed her sentiments. She remembered vividly one day when she broached the subject of how she was feeling with him. He had listened attentively, and then he had placed a hand on hers.

"Love of my life ... The mysteries of life are plenty. And sometimes, we shouldn't try explaining it. I understand how you're feeling, and I appreciate the fact that you have come to me with this. I guess we will just have to wait till you're a little older and then we will have this conversation again because we can't be sure of the situation until you're old enough to really understand it."

His words, for some reason, helped calm her down. The fact that he took the time to understand her and her doubts. It made her feel heard, understood, and cherished. She nodded. And she had slept better that day. In fact, the period right after that conversation was the longest that she went through without actively thinking about it.

"I'm going to see grandad upstairs!" she shouted out to everyone. Then she went her way. At his door, she paused and knocked lightly, then pushed the door open and went in. He was sitting at his desk, looking out the window into the gardens. The room was well aerated and bright.

"Grandad!" she called out to him excitedly. He looked around and squinted. He was wearing his usual grey pullover over a light blue shirt.

"Love of my life!" he said as his wrinkled face broke into a smile.

"Oh, grandad!" she said as she flung her arms around his neck.

"I hear your grandma blackmailed you into coming home again!" he said with a weak laugh.

"She didn't need to. I already missed you so much!" she said.

"How are you?" he asked.

His voice told her that he wasn't expecting a generic answer. He wanted the truth.

"I feel a little lost sometimes." She replied.

"Sometimes I feel like I can't breathe. I don't know why, but it feels like everything is not right".

She launched into a long story about everything she had been going through emotionally. She told him about how she had been having nightmares. She went as far as telling him about everything she had experienced on her tours. He listened. He was her listener, mentor and guide and until recently, when he was diagnosed with Alzheimer's, he was also her big personal guard. They shared a sweet and emotional bond. But, presently, he looked at her with a sad, faraway look in his eyes.

"Klara... Oh! Klara, where have you been?"

She was a little taken aback by his words. Then, of course, she remembered Klara. He had mentioned her once or twice a very long time ago. He had said to her:

"You remind me of a girl from long ago. She was a housekeeper in my brother's house. She was

Hungarian... I think." He seemed to think about it for a little while and then he added:

"Long golden hair like yours and very delicate look. Her name was Klara...

There was a staring look in his eyes as he talked about this woman Klara. She must have been pretty remarkable if he remembered her after so many years. Presently, it struck her that he had mentioned that the so-called Klara was Hungarian. What were the odds? She had not even remembered until this moment when he called her by the lady's name. She knew that he said she reminded him of Klara. But it had never occurred to her that he meant that she physically looked like Klara. She found the coincidence funny and unsettling the same. What were the odds that a Hungarian maid would look exactly like her and she has herself this special bond with Hungary?

"Does Klara look like me?" she asked. He looked at her for a while, and then he frowned.

"Of course Klara looks like you ... you're Klara!"

She sighed. His mistake was upsetting.

"... Do you know where I can find Klara right now, Grandad?"

"Hungary!" he laughed. It was all he could say before he seemed to lose touch with reality again. She swallowed hard and stood up to leave the room.

"Are you leaving Klara?" he called out.

"I'll be back!" she replied.

Part 4

At the hospital

The waiting part was the worst, right behind the part where she had even to convince herself that she needed to take a DNA test. She was scared that she would be right, and she was even more scared that she would be wrong. If the DNA test confirmed what her parents had always told her, that she was their child... then it would mean that she had spent most of her life doubting her parents. It would mean that there is something wrong with her. Something so intense that she would feel like she belonged to the wrong family and culture.

She had mailed the DNA samples from her parents and herself with shaking hands. She opened the package that she got back with her heart going so fast that she was sure it would burst out of her chest. She pulled the results out and took several deep breaths before looking down at them. With the results in her hand, her head filled up with all emotions and scenarios; she didn't need to be an expert to know what the results said. Neither of her parents was a blood relative of hers. But since her parents were so sure that they were her parents, she figured that the problem was probably not them.

The answer to her question was not going to be found in their home. It was going to be found in the hospital where she had been born because it was the only layover between when her mother was pregnant and when they brought home a baby. She needed now more than ever to go back to the hospital where she was born. At the moment, she was not interested in who was guilty. It was not about who did what. She just wanted to know what happened and how she came to be with people who were not her biological parents. She didn't want a fight; she wanted the truth.

She was staring into space, fiddling with her bracelet, as she waited for the arrival of the hospital director.

Her face was set into a permanent blank look. It had taken her almost 40 years to get to this point. But sitting in that chair that day, she knew that there was no turning back. There were just too many questions unanswered. And at that moment, she did not care who got hurt or what happened anymore. She was determined to find a solution to the problem once and for all. The room was brightly painted in a combination of blue and white. It did not feel like a hospital. The room could have been located in any kind of office building. The door opened, and a lady of about 50 years old walked in.

"Thank you for your patience; I understand that you have some questions and possible complaints about the hospital, and I am here to be of assistance. Please tell me, how may we be of help to you today?" The lady asked with a very broad smile that appeared friendly but really was not.

She had rehearsed this conversation in her mind repeatedly, but now that she was sitting in front of someone who could make a difference, she found herself slightly tongue-tied. She was almost 40 years old, and she did not even know where to start especially seeing that most of the things she had to say were based on speculation and guesswork... some were also based on her personal feelings and emotions over the years.

"I was born in this exact hospital about 40 years ago." She said with a wistful smile.

"Oh really... that is so nice." The hospital director said. But Alexandra still did not feel at ease. Something in the air told her that she was not welcome. Something that was charged and resentful.

The lady had been staring at her computer screen all the while as Sasha made her little speech.

"Yes... Indeed" she said...

"Right"

"I do not believe I belong with the family that took me home as their baby from this hospital. It is likely my real family had a baby girl right next door to me on the night that I was born. I don't know if it was intentional or a mistake, but I know that my parents went home with the wrong baby that night. I know because I have taken a DNA test that proves I'm not their child, even though they took me home from this hospital that night. I am trying to locate my biological family, and I was hoping to get their name and address from this hospital if you just check your records and figure out who was placed in the room next to my family's that night."

Her words were concise and straight-forward, and she hoped that this would help convince the director to help her without a fuss. But even before the tight ponytail lady opened her mouth, Alexandra knew precisely what would happen.

"If I understand you correctly, you were born in this hospital over 40 years ago and recently discovered that you do not share DNA with the people who raised you?"

"Yes, that's correct," Alexandra said.

The woman looked at her with what appeared like disdain. Sasha didn't like her very much. But she knew that the only way she was ever going to get real answers to her questions was if she maintained her calm.

"Look, I understand everything you have described, and I sympathize with you because it is really important for people to get closure for every trauma they experience. But I really can't help you because hospital policies say that..."

Alexandra did not let her finish, and she almost laughed.

"Yes, yes, I'm aware of your hospital policies and I'm also aware that the last thing your hospital needs is a lawsuit right now because you're struggling financially. I know some sort of error was made but don't underestimate my ability to make the entire world believe that the error was intentional and sue you for all the distress that this intentional error caused me and my family."

Even though she was saying something as serious as a lawsuit, Alexandra's face remained straight and calm, and she was even smiling as she delivered her lines.

"Listen, I don't want any trouble. I understand that you're a very busy woman and I respect that. But this is something that I really want to do. We can both save each other a lot of stress. You don't need to give me the hospital records or patient records; I just need the person's name in the next room the night I was born".

The hospital director looked into her computer one last time. She appeared to be weighing the pros and cons and figuring out if there was any way to get out of this conversation. She must have decided otherwise because she reached for the phone on her desk and made a call.

About 5 minutes later, Sasha had right in her hands the full name and address of the couple that had the baby next door that night.

She stayed there for several seconds, just staring at that piece of paper. She was getting much closer, and she suddenly felt a wave of panic. One thing was to locate and identify her biological parents. Whether or not they'll be happy with the information they were about to receive was another conversation entirely. So, she could feel her heart pounding extremely fast in her chest, and even as she stood up and said her goodbyes to the lady, she left the room without adding any more words.

She looked down at the address that came with the name and her eyes widened from shock and surprise. The address was only a few miles from her parents' house. She had spent so long in the shadow of Venice's palaces and canals, living right across from her biological parents and now... she couldn't wait to visit them and finally find out who and what they were. But she was also somewhat scared. She had spent such a long time worrying over whether or not they would like her.

Even if she was theirs by biology, she was not the child they raised. They were bound to be differences, and she just didn't know how that was supposed to go. The fact that she was already in Italy meant that she could go over there almost immediately and knock on their door. Her heart was in her mouth, and she could barely breathe as she made the decision to check it out right away.

The address that she was given was less than ten minutes away.

It was so eerily close that she had to take several deep breaths as she started to feel panic one moment and euphoria the next.

She drove right over there as though her life depended on it. She barely drove within the speed limit. She was to visit her biological parents and potentially fix all these problems.

If there was anything that she knew about human nature, she knew that it was highly likely that there would be some sort of rivalry between her and whatever child it was they had raised as their own. The truth is that she didn't really mind... but she hoped that they would have a good relationship.

"You reached your destination," the satnav said.

She looked out her car window and couldn't believe her eyes. She knew the house. She remembered the house vividly, and she almost couldn't believe that it had been there all the while. That they had been there all the time.

"Over there? Just over there?" she found herself saying as she tried to figure out the family that lived there. She had lovely memories of riding her bike past that house in springtime or just enjoying the early winter snow. She remembered waving at a figure in the door once. A dark-haired, long-limbed kid of around eight years old, it was the only memory she had of that family.

She almost instantly began a long self-deprecating tirade.

"I am such a coward... what would it cost to go in and tell them everything I know? How hard can that be?" but she knew it was hard. Hard enough to make her throat suddenly feel dry.

She stepped out of her car and looked up at the house. Taking in its beauty for the first time... She had viewed it in the light of how close it was to the property she had grown up in. She had considered it in the light of the fact that she had spent most of her childhood just minutes away from her birth parents and had never been the wiser. She drew a big breath, rubbed her palms together, and blew out the air through her mouth. Her mother would have laughed if she had been there. She could hear the beautiful, rich voice in her head...

She sighed as she walked up to the front door. She knew that she had already taken the first steps and now she could not wait to see how everything turned out. But at the same time, there was a deep feeling of fear in her. It was as though she could not breathe and couldn't talk or move simultaneously.

She wanted to run all the way to the porch and demand that the occupants come out right away. In the same breath, she wanted to turn around and make a dash for it. She wanted to run so far away that she would be away from everything that could remind her of her present circumstances.

At the front of the house, she knocked on the door and waited for a few seconds to pass before knocking again. Then, just as she was about to hit the third time, the door swung open on an elderly woman of about 70 years old who stood there.

She took several moments to get back her composure.

When eventually she felt steady enough to talk, she opened her mouth, and nothing came out. Thus, to save her dignity, she thrust her phone with the address on it into the older woman's hands. She looked down at the address and read it for a few seconds but when she saw the name at the top of it, she smiled and shook her head.

"I'm so sorry, my dear," the woman said with a sad smile.

"But they have moved away from here; it's been many years."

Whatever hopes Sasha had cultivated before she got to that front door had instantly been squashed. To think that she had gone to all that trouble just to get to that place at that moment and be told that the reason she had gone through all that stress could not even be fulfilled.

It was excruciating, and the woman must have seen her face because she put a hand on her shoulder.

"Dear, they moved away, but I still have their new address if you like."

"Yes, yes, please give me the address" Sasha said.

The woman smiled again and turned into the house. She returned minutes later with a piece of paper on which she had written the address.

"Here. Take it. I hope you find what you're looking for".

"Thank you, thank you so much", she said as she started to leave.

When she got back to her car, she just sat in there for a moment and cried. There were so many emotions going through her body that she could not even explain anymore. Even though her parents loved her very much, she couldn't think of a way to make them understand how she felt, and this had always been a problem between them.

They were convinced that she was their daughter. After all, they brought her home together from the hospital.

She held the piece of paper and looked into it one more time.

Kovács Jenő and Magda

45 Krisztina Körút Budapest.

The address that stared back at her was one that she was well familiar with. The time she had spent in Budapest had allowed her to see a lot of the city. More importantly, she knew this address because her favourite hotel was on that same street. It was the same hotel she had used for years, and it had never even occurred to her that her family might be anywhere nearby. She could feel her heart racing. With shaking hands, she booked her flight immediately, using her mobile phone. She needed answers and was not going to take any chances with it.

Part 5

"Eastern songs are more beautiful, and anyone with a heart who listens to them   will be moved to tears."

-Joseph Roth

The flight seemed to last forever. It definitely took too long. Every moment felt like years to her as she constantly checked her watch. The passenger seated next to her wanted to make some kind of conversation, but all Alexandra desired was to be left with her thoughts. She didn't want anyone to spoil that moment, that special journey.

Everything she did to distract herself did not work, and she was starting to feel restless when the flight eventually landed. She got off the airplane feeling like she was ready to run all the way. She just couldn't stop thinking about what was about to happen and how her life was about to change. Forever. At intervals, she found herself wondering if she was doing the right thing. She can just go back and move on with her life right after she confirms whether or not they are her real parents. Because what was the point of usurping their lives now? She spent most of her life in doubt especially concerning her paternity and identity. It is one thing to doubt your paternity and identity; it was entirely a different ball game when it became a reality.

She quickly got in one of the taxis parked outside the international arrivals. It was a hot, sunny day.

She only had light travel luggage.

Sasha had convinced herself that she needed to know. But this moment, she found herself wondering. Did she? Did you really need to go in there and potentially destroy everyone's lives just by giving them this information? Nearly every step of the way until she got to her destination, she found herself wondering what would happen if they rejected her. But she didn't come back. She kept on her journey because she had no other choice. Forty years is a long time to be unsure. A ridiculously long time to live knowing that you do not belong in the world you've been put in.

Her plan was all laid out in her now complicated mind. She wasn't going to lie; she would use the legitimate excuse that… her grandfather knew a Hungarian lady in Venice and believed she could be related to them. Yes, perhaps a little stretched out as an excuse, but she needed this link between Venice and Budapest, at least for them to let her in their house and ultimately, in their lives.

The trees moved past extremely fast, and the closer she got to her destination, the more apprehensive she was. But somehow, she found the strength to choose to keep going even when she felt like she was doing the absolute wrong thing. The taxi rolled to a slow stop.

The building was plain. A four-storey building. Nothing like the castle she grew up in. It was yellow and looked like it belonged to her history books. But she liked it. She had always liked it even though she had never looked at it the way she presently did.

She stood outside the yellow walled building, breathing heavily and trying to compose herself.

Looking at those little balconies that have seen more history than plant pots, the Hungarian flags were proudly swirling in the light breeze and this ultimate coincidence made her smile. "Italian and Hungarian flags have the same colours, just a different layout," she whispered. Sasha turned around and looked at the opposite direction. It was a breathtaking view over Vérmező Park, and she allowed herself to soak in its beauty. This part of town had always fascinated her, even when she didn't know that this family lived there. The sun hit the floor, and the trees made her want to bask around that place even though she hated the sun. Maybe it was just a subconscious attempt to delay the inevitable. But there she was. After standing there for several moments, she turned around and pressed the doorbell at the name Kovács. Maybe 8 or 10 families lived there. The door opened. In just a few moments, she will hear voices coming from the 3rd floor. It wasn't till that moment that she realised she had been silently hoping they wouldn't be in. But they were home and with an unsure pace, she climbed the flights of stairs. The staircase walls are grey, and there are plant pots on every floor. A welcoming feeling invaded her.

The door opened, and a middle-aged lady stood there. The face was neither hostile nor friendly.

She was wearing a green skirt below her knees and too big for her.

A lovely light brown shirt. She couldn't see the patterns as she wore an apron covering the front, which she removed immediately.

"She must be cooking," Sasha thought.

"Yes. Can I help you?" The lady said in Hungarian.

Sasha stood there for a little bit before she replied in perfect Hungarian:

"Good morning. My name is Sasha." The woman glared at her. At first, with some indifference. Then there was some interest on her face.

"Okay, Sasha. How may I help you?" She asked.

Sasha looked down. And then into the woman's face. She finally found a voice and spoke.

"I am so sorry to bother you and your family. I come from Italy, from Venice actually, and I believe you know my grandparents."

The woman looked at Sasha and frowned.

"Your grandparents?" The woman asked just to be precise.

"Yes, yes," Sasha answered.

She invited in. She then called her husband.

In the living room, she motioned for Sasha to sit down.

The apartment was humble, dated, with the smell of cabbage on the cooker, but she could tell that they were incredibly lovely and caring people. The room was well lit with natural light coming through the windows. There were multiple flower vases on the windowsill.

As she sat there, she couldn't help but sense a feeling of cosiness.

The sofas were soft from use, which somehow seemed to have made them even more comfortable. And that smell of cabbage stew on the cooker made the house even more homely.

Sasha took several deep breaths in an attempt to compose herself for what she was about to tell. The deep breaths filled her nostrils with the smell of home, something that she deeply appreciated at that moment.

The couple sat there. Sasha started her story... "Do you have a person called Klára in your family, significantly older, that lived in Italy?"

"Yes... My mother!" Mrs. Kovács said.

Sasha knew that everything she was saying must have sounded so crazy. But she could also tell from how they looked at her that they believed her. She didn't know why they believed her, but she could tell that they did.

"Well, I'm pleased I am in the right place. My grandfather was right; Klára worked for his brother in Venice". She spoke. Mrs. Kovács's face lit up with a pleasant smile.

"Oh, what a wonderful coincidence, we moved there too in our 20s, isn't it, Jenő?"

She kindly said, turning to her husband.

He nodded.

He is a Professor at Budapest University, she gathered. Sasha looked around and smiled a little, feeling very comfortable but tempted to walk around the apartment. There was a long wall with a bookcase attached. It had way more books than a small bookshop, old books that had infused their sweet smell into the house. The smell of books was heady and mind filling. They looked so old and so neatly handled that there was barely any wear on most of them, even though it was obvious that they had existed for a long time.

Sasha always felt so happy and overwhelmed by the smell and the beauty of books, especially the old ones. There was something in them that made her feel limitless. She found herself staring, glaring at the books in hopes of catching titles and authors. It would seem that the reasonable thing to do was to ask if she could explore the bookshelves, but lots of emotions were running through her body and she just stared at the books instead. Most of them were written in Hungarian, and she found that as much as her sight would allow her to catch the letters, she could read the titles.

To her far left was a different wall. This one was well adorned with paintings. It wasn't the only wall with paintings, but it was the only one with that many paintings so close together.

The room's wallpaper was dark, with big yellow flowers as the pattern. Yet, the room gave off feelings of comfort never experienced before—a sense of belonging.

She felt warm-hearted by their welcome as they remember their life in Venice, talking about their first trip on the gondola, their jobs in a totally new country and culture. And their return to Hungary, to their roots, as they proudly stated.

Mrs. Kovács was smiling; her husband went onto the balcony.

Sasha could literally see her hotel room window when he opened the balcony door. "Crazy," she thought, finding herself in the house that she often overlooked when daydreaming or just looking out at night at the yellow tram 56 passing by.

"I will bring some tea" Mrs. Kovács said. Sasha watched as she left the room. Even though the Kovács had not kicked her out of their home, she still couldn't say with confidence that she had been accepted into their home, much less their lives. She knew this was a long process and she needed to approach the situation in a calm, thoughtful manner. Mr. Kovács looked away from her the whole time his wife was away.

She looked up a couple of times, looked around... She is also trying to avoid appearing like she's forcing eye contact. It was bad enough that she had come into their home to talk. She felt sinking on that sofa. Thankfully, she didn't have to wait too long before his wife returned to the room. She brought in a tea set of delicate Zsolnay porcelain on a wooden tray. Beautiful hand-painted delicate roses covered the teapot and the little teacups.

She looked in the man's direction for the first time since his wife had left the room. That was when she saw it.

It's sat there on the mantelpiece just behind him. The eyes glittered and the smile was big. The cheeks were round and rosy, beautiful long black hair framing the entirety of the face and a long elegant neck. There were no questions to be asked. This girl was definitely her parents' daughter. She was the exact likeness of her mother, with that smile looking like it had been cut out of one of her mother's older pictures. It was all Sasha could do to not burst into tears as she stared at the photo. Her throat started to hurt and felt very tight.

"Is that your daughter?" She asked as she pointed at the picture.

"Yes. Yes, she is"

"She was 12 in that photo..." Mrs. Kovács said. Sasha found herself glaring at the picture. She couldn't tell what colour the girl's eyes were, but she could see the long jet-black hair, the long eyebrows and lashes and that beautiful smile. The girl was tall... definitely taller than the average twelve-year-old. She was a beauty with a smile that would melt hearts. Sasha knew precisely where that smile came from. It was as though someone had cut a picture of her father's smiling lips and pasted it on the younger girl's picture. Her tanned skin tone told Sasha that this was a girl who loved the outdoors. But perhaps what sealed it all for her was that poise.

There was something about it. Something told her that this was a female version of her father, with all the beauty of his face and her mother's grace. As much as Sasha tried to pull her gaze away, she couldn't.

Magda seemed to notice because she touched Sasha's hand gently.

"Are you okay?" she asked. Sasha jerked just a little as she was pulled out of her thoughts and said:

"Lovely picture... she is so beautiful." Sasha reply. Neither of them responded, and Sasha wondered why.

With perhaps excessive curiosity, she asked:

"Does she live in the city too?"

And before either of them could answer, she continued:

"Will I be able to see her? It would be great to meet her"

By the time she was done talking, Mrs. Kovács was already crying, and she just sat there wondering what she had said or done wrong.

And perhaps because his wife was crying, Mr. Kovács's eyes filled up with tears. At this point, she didn't know what to say or do.

"We lost her many years ago."

Sasha stood there in disbelief.

Mr. Kovács repeated what his wife had said.

"Tanya...she's no longer with us; she died when she was 13.... car accident."

For once in her life, Sasha was speechless and tried hard not to break down too.

"I am... I am so sorry..." was all she could say.

She sat there frozen. Their daughter was dead... Which also meant that her parent's daughter was dead. The girl with the beautiful long hair was dead... Sasha pinched herself a couple of times and was still too weak to stand up. At that moment, she felt like she had made a huge mistake. If she had ever taken into consideration the fact that the other girl might be dead, she probably would never have contacted this family about what happened to their babies at birth. As much as she didn't like to admit it, it was apparent to her now that everything had changed. She didn't need a DNA test to know that she belonged to this family. That look was unmistakable.

She was the spitting image of everything that she needed to be to belong in that family. If she was ever confused about how this happened, that wasn't the case anymore, as it had become obvious that the babies had been swapped at birth. A horrendous utterly sad, tragic mistake. She wasn't sure what exactly happened or why it happened, nor was she so sure whether it was intentional. But there she was, at 11.30 in the morning, sitting in this couple's living room and prepared to tell them that she was the daughter who had been swapped at birth with another couple's child. With a suffocating feeling in her chest, she suddenly felt an intense urge to leave the room and realized the gravity of what she had uncovered. The can of worms she had opened meant that she had to tell her parents that their real biological child was dead. That not only their child has been stolen from them, but they were also never going to see the child again. Sasha's heart suddenly felt so heavy in her chest. She stood up shakily and forced a smile.

"I had no idea. I'm sorry about all of this. I'll try to come back and see you before I go back to Italy." She said. The Kovács didn't seem to mind even through their sadness. They remained welcoming and lovely. Magda smiled through her tears and patted Sasha on the back. "It's okay."

"I'm so sorry to have stormed into your life like this; I think I better go now," she said as she made her way to the front door, long before the couple could keep up with her. Tears filled her eyes; she ran down the stairs and stumbled blindly into the sunlight.

Instead of going back to her hotel, she decided to walk to the Fisherman's Bastion. She knew by heart every step, passing Mikó Utca and up to those steep stairs. But, as much as she tried, she couldn't control herself and burst into tears.

She pulled her arms to cover her face and cried uncontrollably. This was a route she used to take on her guided tours loud with laughter, showing everyone the beauty of Budapest. Now she was taking that same route, with only her tears for company.

Once she arrived at the top, there was only an unbearable silence, and she was alone with an immensely heavy secret. She could not take her mind off the fact that a biological parent looked exactly like her. She didn't need to ask any questions. The moment that woman opened the door, she knew who she was. She could immediately see the resemblance between herself and the man she had just found. She had a similar profile as her dad, a man so handsome, not so tall, and well-built that he could have been mistaken for a fit fifty-year-old. Like herself, with smiling eyes and her mother's hair and pale skin, just like her own complexion, petite with a sadness in her eyes.

"Tanya. Tanya Kovács". She repeated a few times, just to hear what that name sounded.

"I was meant to be called Tanya! I was born Tanya Kovács! My mother must have whispered that name to my ear just after my birth, briefly holding me, just before I was taken from her arms into the intensive care unit."

Considering the fact that the mission she had come for was accomplished, she felt like she should be happy. She was elated at the idea of having found biological parents in the end. Leaving their home, however, she was in pieces.

How was she supposed to face appearance in Italy, knowing what she had uncovered?

Was she even supposed to tell the truth under these circumstances?

One couple will be happy to know that their biological daughter is alive, but they have grieved for someone else daughter for 27 years. Another couple will lose their daughter and have already lost their real one.

That night, Sasha realized that whatever she thought she would find when she set out to look for her family, this was not it. And this was definitely not some news she wanted to be giving anybody, much less the family that raised and loved her deeply till this point.

She felt so alone. No one to share that big secret. Alone to carry the weight of this sad news. Not a shoulder to cry on.

Part 6

"*Budapest is profoundly the city of love. Believe me, those who really know this town can only speak with tears in their eyes.*"

-Szerb Antal

The following day, she remained in her hotel room, tried to pull herself together, numbed, thinking about everything that had happened. She rescheduled her flight sooner than planned.

Sasha then went for a walk where her heart took her. To find peace, to reflect.

"Surely Tanya would have come here; she saw what I'm seeing now". Magda and Jenő Kovács were a sweet, amazing couple and now she had hurt them and was leaving. The temptation to leave without telling the truth to the Kovács was very high. Or even if it was just to go and say goodbye. But there was also the fact that she had promised them that she would come back. So when she was ready to leave, she packed up and decided to go over to their apartment.

She got back to the yellow walls with mixed feelings. And this time, when she pressed the doorbell, a male voice answered. A voice she hasn't heard before. The door opened a few moments later, and a young man was standing there. And she intuitively knew who he was.

She followed him. But by the time they got into the living room, she wanted to tell exactly who she was. She didn't really see his eyes through the thick lenses he wore. But you could tell that his eyes were brown, just like her own.

"Magda. It's so nice to see you again", she said and they hugged.

Magda stepped backward and turned to look at the man.

"Let me introduce you to Gábor, our son".

Sasha could tell that he was a very well-mannered elegant man in his early 30s. His face was pleasant to look at and when he smiled, he had little dimples.

His glasses shifted just a little bit and he had to push them back up his nose correctly. That split second allowed her to see his beautiful brown eyes and she found herself smiling at him.

"Gábor, meet Miss Sasha."

Gábor removed the pipe he was smoking and made his way toward her. His smile was full and sincere.

"Csókolom" and kissed the back of her hand.

She wanted to hug him like a long-lost brother, tell him she was home now. And she would take care of him but that would be silly, wouldn't it? After all, he was a grown man at that point. So instead, she settled for allowing him to place that kiss on the back of her hand.

He went over to a corner where there was a high chair and started to play the clarinet softly. She sat down with a cup of tea. She could hear Gábor playing one of those melancholic tzigane melodies and she began to feel lots of emotion within her, making her want to cry.

Every single note carried emotions that could never be expressed in words. And she found herself feeling it along with him. There was no doubt about it. She felt a strong connexion with Gábor. It was a sweet, protective feeling mixed with a sense of family and love.

Gábor made a lasting impression on her. He looked like someone out of a 40s movie with his unique dress code, which made her smile. The glasses on his nose made him cute, but he would be even more handsome without them.

"Sasha, would you like to come for a drink where I am playing the clarinet with my friends at the nearby Déryné Bisztró?"

And that was when it clicked in her mind. She had seen Gábor before, that restaurant... She knew his face, his playing, and his sweet smile. But this was the first time it was occurring to her that they had strikingly similar features.

"I'm sure I have seen you there before," she exclaimed. She knew, because she was used to frequent that beautiful, romantic, vibrant place just right down the street from her hotel. The conversation between them from that point onwards was unrestrained. And she found that she was not just invited for lunch but also for dinner the next day. Yet, they met that same evening again. She ended up staying longer than she planned. She realised that her life was coming together with intense pain and happiness.

Part 7

"We cannot change the past, but we can reshape the future."

Dalai Lama

September, between Budapest and Venice

She stood by the window, looking out at those clouds. The flight was smooth and lost in her thoughts; the question "what now" had continued to ring in her mind all throughout the journey. She had gone out of her way to find her birth parents, and now that she had found what she was looking for, she had no idea what to do with the information. Was this the point where she was supposed to go back home and tell her parents what had happened? How exactly was she supposed to approach them and tell them that she had found their real daughter, but she was now dead? As much as she knew that she was different from her parents, she couldn't deny that they gave her their best. To the best of their abilities, they were kind and honest, but perhaps most importantly, they were able to provide her with a lot of love. And they have always been there for her.

Her parents had made sure she knew everything concerning finances, business, and everything else. But, because she was their only child, they found it necessary to make sure that she understood the rudiments of the business so that she could take over from them at some point in the future.

And even though she's 40 years old, she still hadn't gotten a need to take over from her parents. She knows that if anything happened to them, the possibility of the business would fall squarely on her shoulders. But, Undauntedly, they had given her a good life. Now she knew that even though this was something she ought to tell them, she knew that she couldn't just tell them because it would shatter their world.

Having considered all the above rhetoric, she finally made the decision to go back to Venice and just promptly resume her life. She would not tell anyone what she knew until she absolutely had to. What they do not hear cannot make them unhappy.

The plan seemed like a good one and easy to follow. Especially since they would not be under the same roof most of the time, she would be able to avoid having that conversation for as long as possible.

She thought she would have the happiness of discovering her real parents but such did not come. She waited to feel ecstatic or like she had achieved something, but it didn't happen. Instead, she felt guilt. Perhaps if the other girl had not died, she would have handled it differently. Maybe they'll be having extended family dinners and having loud, happy conversations in their homes by now. She had prepared herself mentally and psychologically for many things, including rejection, hatred, and denial. But she had never prepared for the possibility that she would not be able to even tell her parents what she had done.

Thus, the period immediately following her homecoming had her locking herself in a hotel room she rented. Despite the stunning view over the beach and the Adriatic Sea, it was as if she was mourning a long-lost friend or lover or maybe sister. And perhaps it was because she had always known within her that if she was with her family, then there was a child somewhere else that had to be her with her family too. And in all of her imaginations, the other girl was not the adversary. The other girl was not the challenge she had to overcome to live happily ever after. Instead, the other girl was just a co victim of a situation they did not plan for. Now it's turned out that she was not only right, but she was also accurate in all her predictions and suspicion. The only thing that destroyed the happiness was that the girl she would have shared her family happily was nowhere to be found. So that night, as she lay in her bed and tried to be calm, she prayed silently for rain and thunderstorms. These were the only things that ever calmed her down. And she desperately wished for it at that moment.

Life became very monotonous for her. She continued to hide from her parents, pretending she was still in Budapest even though she had been back in Italy for two weeks now. She was not ready to face them, not prepared to face the consequences of what she had done. But perhaps more importantly, she was not ready to face herself... And having lived her life up to this point as a single woman, she didn't even want any man in her space to share her grief with.

After what seemed like forever being a hermit, she decided she couldn't live like this anymore. It was not her fault that the Kovács' daughter died. But it was going to be her fault if Sasha died too. She made a decision. She was going back to Budapest. She owed her parents love and affection, and that was what they were going to get from her. But she also owed herself a good and fulfilled life in the country she loved so much. And that was precisely what she was going to get. So, once again, packed in a bag, and this time around, she knew exactly where she was going and what she was going to do

Part 8

"Autumn and Buda were born of the same mother. "

Krudy Gyula

Budapest, October

The city of Budapest held a new meaning for her today. It was not just the random city that made her feel good or with which she connected. It was a hometown, her family's home, for generations and generations. It was where all her ancestors were buried and where her family lived today. This was the home of her culture, of her people. But perhaps most importantly, this was the place where she found herself. So as the taxi drove through the city, she looked at it with brand new eyes.

Seeing things that she usually would not have noticed before and falling in love with them all over again. She smiled, looking at the beautiful Széchenyi Bath yellow curvy building. She knew exactly where to go and how to get there. And this time around, she also knew exactly what to expect when she did get there. Gábor was her brother, and even if they had not being raised by the same parents, they shared the same blood. Also, she had always wanted one of those childhoods where she would get a younger brother or sister with whom she would play or fight. Someone to run to when the entire world was against her, who would support her even if she was wrong.

But all of her life, not once had it ever really occurred to her that she was lonely and craving a different family structure until now. Now that she could see what she could have had. A father and mother living a simple life, with a brother who played the clarinet and kissed the back of her hand... This was something to crave for. Something to desire and she decided to forgive herself for craving it and reaching for it.

There she was now, only a few steps away. She could see the red canopy outside the buzzing Bistro and those little lights. What a wonderful place. She could hear the music all the way from outside the building. It was beautiful. She saw a few people passing by and she wanted to call their attention to let them know that the man playing the clarinet was her brother. She was filled with pride. When she set out to Budapest that day, it had not occurred to her that she would make the decision she was about to make at that moment. She stood out there, listening to the music; she slowly walked towards the entrance, knowing fully well what she would see but still feeling like her breath was taken. When she finally saw him, she remained standing at the entrance, looking across the soft red lights and staring at him. It was at that moment that she knew that she had to move back to Budapest. She was never going to be contented with just coming over whenever she felt like it. This was Her city, and this was Her family. Standing right there she realised that Gábor would be playing there every Saturday night, and she wanted to be right there too, listening and watching him play.

He looked up and saw her; he waved; a sweet spread of happiness filled his face as he made eye contact with her. There was no doubt about it. He was also happy to see her.

He was wearing a nice dark grey suit and tie, and his black-framed glasses, too big for his nose. He looked great with his fedora. Sasha was overwhelmed. She looked stunning in her black dress, high black heels, and the cascade of hair châtain clair.

Déryné was full of music lovers, wine lovers, or simply lovers. She remained standing till he rounded up his "Autumn's leaves." Oh, how she loved that song! She felt a tear running down her velvety skin. He signalled a waiter who brought them a bottle of Tokaji. They drank it, then he went outside to smoke his pipe. The tram 56 passed, carrying barely any passengers on this cold evening.

He came back and said to her:

"I know some really nice places you'd like to see at night. So if you are feeling up to it, I could take you sightseeing tonight." She looked up.

"Come, let's go." He spoke.

And so off they went into the night. The first place he took her to was Krisztina church just across the road. Even though she was well familiar with this location, she had never been inside.

They walked up to Buda Hill. Everything was now closed; they passed the Post Office, headed to Tóth Árpád promenade, and sat on its benches.

They sat there, talking for hours through the night.

"You play the clarinet really well..." She broke into his thoughts. He laughed.

"I know ... I started learning when I was a child. We are a musical family." She smiled as she remembered her own childhood. Her dad had tried to interest her to play the violin to no avail. She was just never interested. Now she wondered if her lack of interest and effort was because she really didn't like music or because the musical instrument, they wanted her to learn was wrong for her.

"I wish I could play..." she mumbled. More for the benefit of hearing herself say it than him. He looked at her with a smile.

"I could teach you and we could play together."

"That will be nice," she said.

"Or maybe I'll learn another instrument to go with the clarinet... And we could..."

"We could start a band!" He finished her sentence for her.

They both looked at each other and burst into laughter.

And from there, they continued to talk. It didn't feel like they were meeting for the second time in their lives. Instead, it felt like they had known each other forever.

"How long are you staying?" Gábor asked suddenly. She could sense some sort of fear in his voice. He wanted to know how deeply invested he should allow himself to be. He wanted to know if this was going to be temporary or if he had many more nights like this to look forwards to. She smiled at him.

"Budapest is really beautiful at night!" she said.

"It's the light." He spoke. She nodded.

"And also... It is home." She looked into his eyes then and he looked back.

"I mean... I'll travel to see my parents sometimes. But this is home, Gábor. I just might be staying," she said.

"Well... Welcome home"

And those were the most beautiful words she had ever heard. She looked at him and his eyes lit up. She broke eye contact, cleared her throat, and looked away.

"Come. We should get you home".

They continued to talk all the way back to her hotel. And then, even afterward, they talked till the early hours in between jazz mood and gypsy songs.

"You know, we should do this again. I know exactly where to take you for the best view over the beautiful Chain Bridge".

She smiled, fighting the urge to tell him what she knew.

"Of course, I would really like that". He kissed her goodnight on the cheek. She turned and unlocked the hotel room door. He hugged her, holding her close to his chest, perhaps too close, and whispered, "you are beautiful."

"Jó éjszakát" he said gently.

"Goodnight, dear Gábor," she said back.

At that precise moment, she understood events were taking another unexpected dimension and a very different meaning, and the truth, till here so well-kept secret, had to come to light.

Behind closed doors, she found herself wondering what the story of Klara really was. Klara, the woman that her grandfather had talked about. For some reason, she was making a connection between the fact that her grandfather was the only one who believed her when she said she didn't feel like she belonged in that life. Furthermore, he was the only one who allowed her to talk to him extensively about her affinity with Hungary. There were too many historical events that she needed to sift through in order to figure out what her purpose in life had to be. But first, all secrets had to come to light.

Part 9

"It's time to start living the life you've imagined."

-Henry James

Venice, November

She sat at her hotel room desk overlooking the window, admiring the seaside. The gentle sound of the waves spreading on the cold wintery beach. "Oh, she sighed, il mare d'inverno, it's so soothing." For the first time since she visited that hospital, she did not feel like she was in a whirlwind. It didn't feel like a dream... or a nightmare. Instead, she was calm and steady. She could see the past clearly, and she was very aware of her present. She knew she would miss Venice, the gondolas, and grandma's beautiful eyes.

There was so much that she wanted to say, so much that she needed to say. Impossible to get it all out on a piece of paper. It was already cowardly enough that she was writing them instead of going over there and just telling them the truth. But her cowardice was not out of disrespect. Instead, it was out of an utmost amount of love for them. And an inability to watch them suffer. There were so many things that she needed to express to them. Like the fact that she didn't think they were inadequate. Or that they had not done well enough for her. They were the parents who raised her, showed her what it meant to love, and how to live in a world like this. They were the ones destined to parent her and they had done a perfect job of it.

The fact that she continued to search for her biological relatives even when there were no real indications of the fact that they weren't, was just instinct and fate.

Because what if her search had not been fruitful? What if one or both of her biological parents were dead and she still found nothing? What if... What if...There were so many things that could have gone wrong for them. And for her too.

She wanted to tell them that she loved them no matter what. That they were the parents that she ever knew. She wanted to thank them for everything that they had done. She wanted them to know that her identity as their child, their daughter, would never change.

She wanted to apologise for every way she might have hurt them. And let them know that it was completely unintentional. There were so many things to say to them. Things that she did not even have the right words for. She sat there and wrote, with her vision blurred by tears.

Dear Mam and Dad,

There are many kinds of love in this world. But nothing surpasses by far the love of the parents to her child. This kind of love is not predicated on anything or anyone really. It is something that is either there or not. It is not negotiable. And you know my lovely, adorable, beautiful parents, you have shown me nothing but the purest form of this. For this, and for everything else, I am grateful.

And nothing will change the fact that you are my parents. You give me love; you give me everything that I am today. So, thank you for that and for all the other things that I am not so conscious of.

I have been your child for forty years but felt like sweet, generous, friendly neighbours were raising me. It was why I always asked whether I was adopted. And why I never could quite fit into the general layout of our family, both biologically and mentally. For forty years, I tried to ignore the way I felt until I couldn't anymore. I had always known the hospital I was born in, and just a little more digging answered the questions I carried for over 40 years.

It breaks my heart to tell you

On the night of mam's delivery, there was a Hungarian woman right next door who also had a baby girl.

That she came out silent and didn't cry right away, which necessitated her being moved to the Neonatal Intensive Care Unit very next to me, and it was in there, the two babies were mistaken one for the other and I was brought to you, and your baby was taken to them.

That neither parent noticed the difference because it all happened so fast.

That you brought me home none the wiser and they took home your child in the same way.

That the child the Hungarian family took home died shortly before her 13th birthday in an automobile accident.

And here we are.

I know this sounds like some horrendous joke but I assure you that I am not joking. All of these facts can be verified through DNA.

I have carried the burden of this information for a few months and now I feel like I must tell you. That I was right to feel the way I felt. And you were also right to feel the way you felt.

A little bit of luck would have been needed for us to figure out what was going on when I was much younger.

I have found this feeling of not belonging, of being a stranger, even in my own home and country, one of the main reasons I was perhaps so withdrawn. I have visited my biological parents once to confirm their identity, and I must say that I don't feel much better. I don't even know for sure if I am better off in my previous state than now. I am so sorry for all and every pain that this will cause.

Mam... I love you. I love what you were to me, for me. I realize that I got a much better life than so many other people and I am grateful that you were part of it. I am so sorry, my dear Mam.

Dad, I love you. Though not biological, you have given me a legacy to be proud of. You have shown me what it means to be a good parent. And I am so pleased to have been a member of your family. None of the information I revealed above will ever change anything for me. You will always be my father. Thank you for not aban-

doning me. Thank you for committing yourself to my development. I got one of the best starts a child could get. And it's all because of you. Thank you so much, Dad.

She sat there, reading and re-reading the letter, trying to find if there was something there that she needed to change. It sounded good enough. She folded it neatly and put it in the envelope. Leaving town was not going to be easy. There were two homes she was about to abandon and even though it was going to be a very painful decision, she knew that it was the right thing for her at that moment.

After explaining to them the tragic error that occurred at the hospital, she continues:

Dear Mr. and Mrs. Kovács,

For 40 years, your heart called me. The same Hungarian blood runs through our veins. I thought about you, even when I didn't know it. My quest for you took me into many things and in a lot of directions. I didn't realise it at the time, but it was you I sought when I came to Hungary in the first place. I didn't know it, but when I became a tour guide, it was because I was hoping I would find you. And I did, in a way. Because for many years, I lodged in the same hotel and stayed in the same room, only to find out recently that that room actually overlooked your front door. I don't know if it is normal for babies to have memories from when they were in their mam's belly. But I know that this is the case with us because I remember you.

I want to apologize for coming into your life the way I did. Because no matter how I choose to say it, I am not your daughter. The fact that you gave me life does not mean that you are my parents, per se. My coming into your life unnecessarily reminded you of the wounds you have had to suffer in losing a child. I admire the life you would have given me. And I am proud to watch Gábor every night at the Bistro playing his clarinet because this is what I always wanted. A simple family with a sibling. Or 2?

Yours is a home that any child would be proud to call its own. The search for my biological family has been something that lasted over 40 years. But I believe it is now time for me to discover myself outside of that search. It is time for me to live a life that is not influenced by what I have lost or what I hope to gain.

Thank you so much for welcoming me into your home without questions. Thank you for opening your heart to me without hesitation.

And once again, she sat back to read her letter. It seemed to cover most of the things she wanted to say. But, it wasn't like there were enough words to express what she was feeling anyway. So, she folded the other letter and put it in an envelope.

There was a heavy feeling in the heart, but she knew what it was. It was that quiet sadness at having to live the way she is. And the anticipation of everything that she is about to get for herself.

When she got on the flight that afternoon, she looked down at Venice disappearing behind the clouds.

The letter for her grandmother is for now, too painful to write.

Maybe she would send a letter to Gábor too. But she wasn't ready. She needed to settle and start her life before paying more attention to the past. With that thought, Alexandra, also known as Sasha..., looked at her bracelet, closed her eyes, and smiled.

A crowded bus journey took her to a small village on the west coast of Lake Balaton.

She rented a pretty little house, hiding from her feelings, pain, fears, and a broken heart.

She still found solace in the Hungarian songs, the rain, and the autumn months. Perhaps one day, she will be able to show others the beauty of a gloomy summer.

Her parents are numbed by life's unfairness, hoping to see and hold Alexandra again.

The Kovács still live in the same apartment, with the same smell of cabbage, and the flowery yellow wallpaper, wishing one day to see her, hug her again, and never let her go.

Gábor is still playing the clarinet and smoking his pipe.

Book cover photo by Benjamin Kövesi

Book cover design by Olivia McCarthy

Printed in Great Britain
by Amazon

80156578R00062